CREEPY HOUSE

Written by: Jennifer May Woods
Illustrated by: Grace Avery-Parkman

To order additional copies of this book, contact:
Xlibris
1-888-795-4274
www.Xlibris.com
Orders@Xlibris.com

To my Favorite Tricker Treater's
Justine, Brett, Derek & Wyatt

There's a big creepy house
at the end of the road

No one goes in,
so it's told...

Creaky stairs make
hairs stand on end

Long dark halls

Cracked walls

old
chandelier
hanging

Wind chimes banging

Rickety picket fence

Falling down

doom and gloom surround

it's quite a sight!

It will give you a fright!

It's Halloween night!

Tricker treating all around

Ghosts and goblins

Running up and down

Superheroes, too

Cotton candy, oh so dandy!

Caramel apples,
brown and sweet

Lollipops galore!

Let's get more!

Laughing, giggling

Tripping while skipping

Through the streets

Edwards Brothers Malloy
Thorofare, NJ USA
May 20, 2015